Fragments of the Universe

Previous Collections by Pat Andrus

Old Woman of Irish Blood

"Pat Andrus is a poet of relationship...*Old Woman* resounds as an outcry of reverence encouraging us to embrace...birth as well as growth, death as well as rebirth...Like their creator, these are poems of spirit and generosity."

~Christianne Balk, author of *Desiring Flight* and *Bindweed*; a recipient of the Walt Whitman Award 1985

"You will not be remiss if you buy, beg, borrow, or steal a copy of Pat Andrus's *Old Woman of Irish Blood.* My copy is already dog-eared...but I will continue to read, peruse and enjoy this poetry for many's the year to come."

~*Ar Mhuin Na Muice: A Journal of Irish News, Literature, Art Politics, Music and Sports*

Fragments of the Universe

Poems

Pat Andrus

2/4/2020

*For Carole,
Who has been an
inspiration, and support
for my own art.
Many Thanks!
On the imagination, always!*

Pat Andrus

BLUE VORTEX PUBLISHERS

Fragments of the Universe
Copyright, © 2019 by Pat Andrus

First Edition
ISBN-13: 978-1-0767-2635-3
ISBN-10: 1-0767-2635-6
10 9 8 7 6 5 4 3 2 1

Published by Blue Vortex Publishers, San Diego, California
bluevortextpublishers.com
bluevortex1@yahoo.com

First paperback printing
Printed in the United States of America
The text in this book is composed in Palatino Linotype

Bingh, Editor
Seretta Martin, Publishing Editor
Clifton King, Technical Editor
Cover: "Untitled blue" painting by Abril Huerta

BLUE VORTEX PUBLISHERS

Acknowledgements:

Grateful acknowledgments to the editors of the following journals and anthologies where certain of these poems, sometimes in earlier versions, first appeared:

Bayou: "Blood Shame Nexus"
California Quarterly: "Son of Xochipilli" & "Erebus No More"
Convergence: "After Roberto Bolaño" & "Ecstasy"
Crosscurrents: "Poem For the Millennium"
　　　　　　　"The Michigan Sonnets"
Haiku Journal: "Crow Haiku"
PMS: "White, With No Apologies"
Scroll: "Let Us Make a Poem"
Waymark – Voices of the Valley: "Upon Viewing 'Night Nude' by
　　　　Steven Mortz," edited by Roger Aplon
A Year In Ink, Vol. 11: "The Rose," edited by Judy Reeves 2018.
Bard Against Hunger: "Send a Hologram to My Stone," edited by
　　　　James P. Wagner (Ishwa), Local Gems Press, 2017.
Beat-itude: "The Knickknacks of Want," edited by James P. Wagner
　　　　(Ishwa), Local Gems Press, 2018.
Blessed "Pests" of the Beloved West: "Black Widow Morning," edited
　　　　by Yvette A. Schnoeker-Shorb and Terril L. Shorb,
　　　　Native West Press, 2003.
The San Diego Poetry Annual, Garden Oaks Press:
　　　　2016-2017, "Chanson Villanelle," &
　　　　2017-2018, "Story" & *2018-2019,* "Lost"
Summation 2017/18: "Upon Viewing 'The Camel's Back' by
　　　　Marjorie Weaver," edited by Robt O'Sullivan Schleith,
　　　　Longboard-to-Tipperary Press in conjunction with Poets inc.
　　　　& Escondido Arts Partnership Municipal Gallery, 2018.

There are many communities and individuals without whose support I would not have completed *Fragments Of the Universe*:

Members of Universal Spirit Center with pastor Rev. Kevin Bucy and gifted artist/music director Amy Steinberg; the Mary and Gary West Senior Center including members of the first hour's Fitness Club with Instructor Patty Frisby at its helm; Crystophver R's, The Poetry Party; the *Thru A Soft Tube* (TAST) reading series at the Wine Lovers with MC Bingh and its many San Diego State University MFAers; and those who shared in the camaraderie and singing voices at the Caliph Bar during karaoke nights before its final closure in late 2018.

Personally, my thanks goes out to Dr. David Luisi and Larry Linton; my sisters Kathy Selivanoff and Peggy Carretta; artist and healing empath Erin Nichole; publisher and long-time friend Anna Johnson; and to Seretta Martin who early on encouraged me to consider publishing my work.

Critical technical support was provided by Carla Reyes; creative cover design by Clifton King, artistic vision by Abril Huerta, and car transport and encouragement by fellow poets Chris Vannoy and Tim Evans.

A special thanks and much gratitude is extended to my editor Bingh, without whose enthusiasm and editing gifts this book would still be "in progress".

And finally, a thank you goes out to a multitude of individuals for their love and encouragement, but unnamed here because of space limitation. Namaste!

A Few Words of Praise:

"When I met Pat Andrus, it was a moment when in our own respective paths, we were looking for other types of expressions to our creativity. We met through dancing—the movements were our words. Pat Andrus's poetry comes from deep inside, bringing the movements of her soul."

> ~**Patricia Greene**, multi-disciplinary artist, has exhibited in the U.S. and Mexico

"*Fragments of the Universe* is a passionate poetic journey deeply engaging us in a lucid realm just outside of time. Our senses are kept wide awake as we find ourselves compelled to reread these important poems, both earthly and spiritual."

> ~**Seretta Martin**, poet, artist, professor, publisher and managing/ regional editor of *San Diego Poetry Annual.*

"Pat Andrus gives poetry license through images of the power to endure, and the depth of meaningful metaphors, always flirting with the infinite and offering an open invitation to join her, without pretense, sitting in contemplation under the Bodhi tree."

> ~ **Crystophver R**, author of *Intellectual Suicide: Poetry to Die For*

Introduction

Opening Pat Andrus's *Fragments of the Universe*, one encounters a creative intelligence, a smart sensitivity, and a sheer commitment to the arts in a woman whose life is richly lived.

Andrus is a wordsmith firmly rooted in her landscape. Whether poetic or political, Andrus leaves her mark: this woman of Irish blood, a mother, mover, activist, and poet in twenty-first century America.

This spangled collection, which spans over two-and-a-half decades, sings. Ecstatic, giddy, the words of "Raptures in Red" nearly fly off the page; or a mother-daughter bonding moment where "I then heard love / inside a baby's throat / crying for milk / for mother's smell / for the lungs of forever"; distraught over the 2016 election results, "where birds / hesitate / to chirp, / or leave their sturdy nests, / in this chaos / of broken moons / of choked thunder": we have a variegated patchwork of autobiography and of the universal.

Flung into the clean spring air in a small room in San Diego, the poems were then collected in the order in which they fell. Accidental—yet with a mysterious logic of the Universe— here they are.

Here, these shiny fragments: "This, you pronounce, / is the end of us," the speaker in "Dénouement" announces, gravely. BUT! But "[i]f tomorrow *is* the day / then bathe me tonight. / Fold me in red silk / before you depart. / I'll wake up tomorrow / and crawl for my soul, / ask my bone spirit / to gather me whole."

~Bingh

For Kira

Table of Contents

Fragments of the Universe

I

Poem

I can't believe
I come inside this open wound.

And the giant under moon,
bringing me to doubt the angels,
where I saw your soul,
your wound of forgiveness.

What makes an open door real?

What claims of magnificence
divide a tree

into the motion of form?
My mother grieves not from the
other side;
and her yellow roses,

asleep from their June growth,
now petal the mornings,

so that you and I remember
the clouds of creation,
the borders of our grown love

Metamorphosis 2

Believe the song
and wild our groan.
When ribbons
and soft lakes gather
their wind
a new angel is born.
Like hollyhocks dreamed
or a raven new,
gold infused,
lifts its wings
toward the sacred air.
And inside its bones,
straightened,
our moon grows over
to the next shore.

Chanson

Sisters came one after another
in baby signs I carved as home.
A pitcher poured one drink most clearly
as I wandered through their songs.

And look, the land was dancing,
crooked words had fallen away.
And meadows grew as yellow
supping up the sun shots
as I danced inside my days.

But my blood ran more quickly
bordering my poetry storms.

Yet yellow was king and queen was purple.
And I was sown in the bosom of hereafter
where I was born.

A Beggar and a Rose

A silent beggar seeks the cosmic soul
One favored lion leads the herd to drink
A rose begins its journey to my core

With savage joy the ravens breed in barns
The blackness of their voices fill the air
A silent beggar seeks the cosmic soul

Grains grown within a field begin to die
A hornet makes its home inside their graves
A rose begins its journey to my core

Delight becomes the tenor of three ghosts
And ancient stars grow silky by the day
A silent beggar seeks the cosmic soul

Three nebulae explode from star's descent
Startling the midst inside one moon's face
A rose begins its journey to my core

The stage is set and blossoms peek through doors
The chorus rushes in to seed the floor
A silent beggar finds his cosmic soul
A rose completes its journey to my core

Upon Viewing 'Ocotillo Sunset' by Patricia Titus

I have found my well:
scarlet into gold into purple.
And soul shapes balance
with a tree's floating leaves
as the whole earth,
lightened with yellow-green scrub,
holds this creation,
with crimson mountains
climbing up the canvas.

What language
encompasses
these emotions
bound in colors
that have no words
to connect the dances
floating through
these universes.
But every day
the birth of all colors
rises before our eyes
as we run, ignorant,
to our next activity,
plan for eternity's
afternoon tea.

Post Election Morning, 2016

Crawl into

the spirit

of me

if you can

stand to hear

sirens

moan and weep.

Be of an oak

and hold my shadow,

though *it* be ever thin

and now

bruises and falls.

Chew on my arm

thirsting even

for chromosomal power.

I want to feel

your mouth,

your teeth,
                    like a king snake

                    hanging onto *its* power
Lovers come and go,

            but you,

                    sing me again

                    our purple dreams.

I need
            your sun

                    to bank

                        my faith

    on this

            post   election   morning,

                    where birds

hesitate

            to chirp,

            or leave their sturdy nests,

                    in this chaos

                            of broken moons
                                of choked thunder.

Compass

Fresh my want
to get into
the bone of me

so I try being whole
patch a piece here
grow new skin there

but if this
is my compass –
your hand cupped
over one breast –
I follow

as your moans
carry us into
blinding
soaked dawns

Command From the Hag of Beara

Bring me down this gothic tale
a basket and a cup of blood
I want to taste with censorious pleasure
the power it holds for love

Like a gold monster I seize your flesh
and then I seize your bones
like burning white barns, animals screaming
where stories from graves scent the loam

I dance on the dirt of the eating hill
I crew every worm passing through
my tongue welcomes gobs of this living earth
to feed my gaping stomach my moon

get afraid hold fast explode in the grass
I can handle your pieces of doom
grow for your fear be true to your mirror
look inside for pictures I poem

mammoth white tusks of ghosts bringing dust
slip mud in my well for a fee
for the storage space gains, losing bones to the crazed
and bodies grow naked dangling

Thalassa's Daughter

~ Upon reading "Gull" by Dolores Kendrick

hand me the sea
to throat this fume
in cold bird language
and stuff foolish ghosts
where fog eats the gulls
their flight grown out
of ocean's spit

Breakup 2

How I danced my days
kept company
with favorite fig trees
traveled to Venice, Beijing, Paris.
Now, stuck inside
creation's stink pile.
And pale moon's dark side?
Just grows in my gut.

I found Eden for three days.
Then the crash.
The placebo burst.
Why did I accept the invite?
Why did I follow Pied Piper
up Moksha's path?

My gold mornings have run amuck.
And streams and mountain peaks,
the ocean's perfect waves –
all dried up.

Some say happiness drowns
after the high; and the paths
leading to magic kingdoms
split into thorny trails.

That point, Time,
makes a mean bargain.
So I fly into the sun.
So I crash sea's solid core.
That rock of dynamite
begs my brain to splinter off.

But no more pandering,
no more tears.
That chapter's closed.
Only the sun can enter now –
with a galaxy's passport,
a nebula's invite.

Upon Viewing "The Camel's Back" by Marjorie Weaver

So mournful, yet steady,
in the shape of
Mohammad's special souls.
I touch the blood-red rug
fronting this canvas,
test its life
with that of the woman
leaning in slight repose
near its surface.

What does she carry,
or own, or desire,
as these dromedaries
of one shade or shape
flank her backside?

She may be the queen
of this camel community
with all her subjects
waiting to serve her
as the sky
shades to midnight
and royal blue air
aids in the peace
of their night dreaming.

But I want in
and wade through
my own night visions
on how to join these beings
with blessings to gain
as the bones
of this painting sing.

Ecstasy

"It is often forgotten that (dictionaries) are artificial repositories, put together well after the languages they define. The roots of language are irrational and of a magical nature."

~ Jorge Luis Borges, Prologue to "El otro, el mismo."

Crawled up your spine last week.
Or was it last night?
The days between your face
and the archangel's mouth.
Oh again, I confuse saints with your breath,
when in a cloud, going across morning midst,
your falcon turns into an eagle.
But did I tell you?
I swam away yesterday,
to a sea stack's lip;
and in the two trees having still survived
on that naked piece of land, that almost pure rock,
rubies dropped from your breasts.
Oh, again a mistake of mornings,
trips, and that dream I carved
in a mountain south of the Equator's north home.
Yes, I bounce, I digress, I look fast
into a river's voice.

Here, though, the bubbling language
placed in tomorrow's sunrise,

I see now.
I see,
and make moons fly
and grace their image
uttered in *your* mouth.

Fellow Comrade

I could be a raging star,
like our own sun on falling granite.
I could languish in death,
the mud pools of my dreams,
found in the daily news.
Or, I could do nothing

except admire
how a newborn kitten pulses out my tears,
or when an oldster
climbs the third floor of a nursing home
just to help an old enemy,
now comrade in survival.

This dance fills my mornings
and keeps me looking up
to the next moon's horizon.

But do you see my happy madness,
wishing *you* good years
beyond my bones even surviving?

Yet I have love flooding the rivers
beyond *my* years to have witnessed.
And you, casing the months for living;
how do your eyes adjust to so many miracles
you witness when your weed
settles into your deepest sights,
like roses dropping their last petals
on the rained sidewalks?

I have no answers
to the blooming cherry tree's exuberance;
nor can I say why the oak and maple

still color their land in September;
or how the abalone's shell
glistens in pearl and sapphire.
But through the emerging sprout
of a single string bean or nasturtium,
you might ask for answers,
or at least get permission
to hum their tunes.
Do it fellow comrade,
do it for your life.

Storyville

There is a violence
in the soft air
a pedigreed air
a place to die only thinly
like bobby pins held together
with just bleached hair.

(And I have no more
the awake tones
to breathe into
this fading soul.)

And old this air, old
the wooden poem
slipped behind the bedroom mirror.
Sunday blues.
Is there any other kind?

I want sweet love
I want scented costumed jackets
I want lemon blossomed air.

But nothing breathes
then breath itself
dissolves
like that lemon tree
growing
until it
drops,
itself dead
in the cold stare.

Ra Invisible

No one
could have delineated
your form as a pharaoh
preaching underground
from your second floor vision.
So I walked through
morning's clean air,
yet could not see
children tousling about
in hide and seeks'
advanced play
you professed
to have shown them.

But go! Lead others
to your sky sun god.
I have a desk waiting
with orchards of poetry
to harvest
before my lone wolf
wakes up again
and howls
at the curious moon.

Warning

I whistle off key.
My hope chest
breeds mosquito eggs.
Look, if you cry too hard,
the oranges, wrapped in cellophane,
rot two months before
the black moon's showing.
And did you really want
my bloodied vagina
taken to forest
the angleworm's trails?

Your seed lifts high its expectations
but my mother
gives her milk away,
as night spirits moan and
refurbish her bed.

Say nothing
and no muskrats will drown
inside your sewer.
But I give no marriage certificate
for infiltrating my den.
It remains holy,
as its dust brims with creation
as your orange leotards
drift outside
my Celtic moons.

Yellow Speak

Tastes like the moon in heat
And smells of flaying limbs
(happy in the sweaty bed!)

Feels like a plastered lemon
(oh drunken, feverish one!)
And sounds like a donkey whispering

But always,
In yellow,
You swim the blood of wheat,
Giddy

Lost

I find strawberries
dangling
from your hair in dreams.
I know it's you
from your scented breath.

I would take your
bone of trust; but
rivers flood canyons
surrounding your cave
and uprooted cedars
block its entrance.

I look for your ribs
in Douglas Firs,
in Hemlocks,
but find not one
on their trunks, their limbs.

So I eat
my language,
and hide its secrets,
that of a woman
soaked in herself,
and far away
from Ireland's Aos Si,
those ancient spirits
who would
sing her home.

Aos Si – Irish name for supernatural race in Irish and Scottish mythology.

Mother

My mother sees me straddle the breeze.
Her ears follow the songs I whistle.
Our evenings soar like a humming bird feast,
like song sparrows filling our hungry breasts.

How does a mother find her language
ripening in one December tune?
The moonrise sets her in that direction.
She's a witch, a balding lover shaping time.

I know these facts about mother.
I made them secure before her death.
Now we share a widening hammock.
Our rivers soak into a violet dusk.

Knickknacks of Want

Saw your name
in a field of sea water,
like an aquatic miracle.
And in a nearby dandelion bed
an expansive root lifted itself up
like a dance unbroken,
keyful,
like the bumblebee's,
the hummingbird's breath –
could break into song.
So I say
move the sky's
and sea's front
to another day
so that we sneak a look
at our own lives
uncensored,
moments filed
in our valley's soul
and brimming
with good luck.

Ecstasy, Take 3

1
if in you, prince
of voluminous awakenings,
one rose and the Word,
honeysuckle soaked.
oh love
lips smile
into beach curves,
wave laughs, and
our dance burning
purple stars.
galaxies blushing
as we touch

2
fiction? no
separation,
walls gone
juniper grows
sweet the corn tassels
clover blooms
around lake's
edges.
to sunfish
swim their fins.
language, and
moon rays
we gulp as
water lilies drift
so pensive
of our breasts.
and shape the
shores, up
from hiding your

beard, my waist
to live, swallow.
oh blossoms
of desire, I fly, your
thighs
wake angels
from sleep.
Love,
hosanna's bell rope.

3
wash of mirrors
your song, fleshed
hungry lips,
open to give;
yet bird of
my heart, adrift.
and half moon
grazing on our souls
where bone bleeds
beads of scar memory;
but tender rose petals
on your pillow
of sleep
and farewell
has lost its
strength in
my blue dreams
of never, forever.

After Betrayal

Forked lightening
splits an oak near your house.
Yet all night you have prayed
for rattlers,
and bats,
an explosion of tornadoes.

The back porch sags.
The morning glories
by 6:00 a.m. wilt.
Shuffling into noon, horses
unreigned, unhaltered,
sniff your front gate.
(This is the story told me
before the action really started.)
Then a banging slips inside
the house's living room.
And there you run,
all seven of you,
before a river
floods the basement,
the sky goes black,
and gladiola stalks
crack open
under the new moon.

Bliss

break me into
shattered coins
and take my poems
all from one stone.
and like daffodils
or lilies of the sun
come walk my words
dedicated to love.

Microscope on Red
        ~ for F.K.

Red deserves lauding
a fire cup of highs
a rainbow of heat
I red my trousers evenings
hot and with class

Red can't be respectable
but gorgeous
yes kingly, queenly, absolutely

I paint my diaries red
even if the days
are blanketed with fog
with brain disasters

Oh but sold red once
its lines getting brutal
its scent a bit on the tiger side

I bake red overtures
when the relatives
get rambunctious
and my cauliflower
has red seeds
growing
from its sternum

Red cheese
at football games
get hefty scores
the loaded muscles peak
the ten forty lines melt

And there you have it
red leaves growing
over your barn
and the sheep
still sleep
and the chickens
speckled
in crimson dots
cluck
their
way
to
Nirvana

November 29, 2018

I come into my day of nights
flesh bound
out of language.
A portent scattered
in my weathered jeans.
How break a solo's sky dive?
How rescue staircase secrets?

I look at you
growing for your reckless days —
a powered keg of hope
dancing job titles
a smoke empty castle.

My children grow
into stars and wandering poets
while I feed storm fugues
brutal song lyrics.
Do the saffron greens
take the stage as I
melt into the lowered songs
grown for my past?

Such are the flowers I compose today
in crooked planked paths
with growls from their backwoods.

No has powers still
and the wrinkled dress
drifts in the breeze
I thought I owned
out from the mountain's
pink throat,
the creeks buried pebbles.

Ruby Throat

Pumpkin seeds sprout
where loam
is drenched with rain;
and granite cracks
into rosary chains,
like a new moon's path
from an old nebula.

I seek scented violets;
and across peach orchards
I carry a song.
In any of my bones crumbling
(where blood has drained),
I simply eat ghost stars.

See the place marked home,
you seekers melting
on a fire's tongue.
There matter grows,
sculpting the air
in sanctified suns.

And children of night
float through sapphire deserts
and warble lullabies
from the full moon's ruby throat.

Seattle's Ode to Sun

Sun demands my sight today
raining its light on the northwest stage

And pilgrims for heat melt at ease
under this star our damp air needs

Could I be summer's attendant host
I'd travel the globe following its force

Now sun deserves our heart our pay
our praise for keeping the dark gods away

Sonnet Unwished For

I was growing my season and caught you there,
still choice as steak, rare, succulent black hair.
But broken shoulders slowing my carefree walk
made engine sounds grinding, without support.
And was that carrion you tossed at my feet
the pavement making soot, masked in the deep?
What hoarse insane screaming blanketed the air?
Your winter's broken promises? Never scarce!
The Bible, the Torah, the Koran set out your bones,
increasing every mountainside to poem
a single line, encased inside its trees.
But I didn't trudge through woods where blue jays weep.
My feet would make no trails into your den.
And you? Just disappeared through a child's grin.

The Face Speaks and the Well Listens

Into the voice all manor of sounds,
lost seasons, hummingbird's first breath;
your sigh, like a call from ocean's own throat.

Have we come to the end yet;
or do frogs summon our croaking,
our place in the vast skies, to make
our lungs chime with the poplar's scent?

I follow your memory until I've exhausted
the pain I baggage in pockets
floating beneath cumulous walls.

But earth, its raw dirt spreading ground,
insists I give voice without whimsy,
no pretty adjectives to decorate speech.

Then river is my teacher, as she carves
her nerves on top boulders and boldly crushes
and cuts objects fronting her trails.

And from river's banks,
you and I link arms, taste our truths
we sometimes speak, to each other,
to the cosmos, saturated no more
with old blood or rainbow jokes.
Just breath
and a commitment to
our past shared Eros,
boned and ready for our feasting
in memory's tender clouds
but still dancing, dancing.

II

Word

grows upward
with its
burnt sienna edges
its cerulean center.

I hold Word
like a wren's feather.

I say to me:
"Lift up Word
and tell it your visions,
your list
of annunciations."

I bring a mirror
to show Word,
and know then
sun power
bathes it
in honey juice
for its depth of soul,
its rays pouring
out its mouth,
settling on its
doved skin.

There within,
the spirit ghosts
dream of creation

and a blood rose
weeps no more.

Psyche

Your soul
stretches
beyond
that
train
you
seize
from
your
morning
dream.
Your
eagle
survives
out of
midnight;
and
underwater
seasons
speed
through
your
glass
moon,
left
on
the
edges
of
this
poem.

Her Amazing Grace

My mother remembers love,
in her piano keys,
through her cherry pudding,
with her children's straight teeth.
I give little to my own
yet she finds it anyway,
grows from it,
gives sweetness back.
And this daughter
must have grown
inside a pearl's clam,
fed the sides of its shell
for her fierce morals.
I can only bless her
and ask forgiveness
before my ashes
settle at the bottom
of their permanent seas.

The Michigan Sonnets

1

The earth swells, rumbling, April's deciduous land.
Our hands darn in a frenzy to find morels.
And the trillium speckle this soggy ground,
this humus factory, dropping white petals on violets
grown vigorous from log's shedding bark.
Mosses sucking dirt and fallen tree limbs,
feed our south swamp, the thick air nursing
our skin and lungs, as we explore its edges.
Mayflowers appear and hold their tender branches,
secure among caked leaves under
jack-in-the pulpits. Sun, faithful all years,
burns off late April rain cover.
And we dance out yet another May Day,
expose our own Dionysian root beds.

2

The piano keys worn but poised coddle old sounds
and the beams above the attic gather the myths.
My child fingers, awkward tiny stubs,
make tingling cracks along the treble clef.
The piano turner purifies notes each autumn
from months of the family's ivory labors.
But body shaking, feet straddled around
the piano bench, I work over scales daily.
The metronome corrects my beats, as
my mother, my grandfather, their heritage
bend over my practice sessions. And no channel
dug in a clover field catches these scales.
I drown no music stands, no Thompson primers,
as I wear down the piano's felt-covered hammers.

3

The furrows, luscious loam, chocolate black.
I eat these earth clots, but for sneering sibling,
and angle worm slimy, wiggling in my mouth.
Spring, and the land gets groomed for rye and barley
to qualify for feeding red delicious next season,
our supposed guardians against farm foreclosures.
Safe now from creeping briars, from rising swamp,
from a water moccasin's sudden exposure,
the acreage curves into summer's first month.
Redwing blackbirds skirt its sprouting edges,
their gurgling notes luring our farm hand Alvie,
who taking his rowboat into evening dusk,
angles for bluegill on Bear and Jeff Lakes,
old piscine matter redolent in their banks.

4

Snow on our land. Snow blinding white our faces.
Snow weighing down barn roofs, the firs' outspread branches.
In a winter extended, drifts fill back roads,
back porches. The land, a white-diamond ocean.
And on its crystal face we make wild geese paths,
and shape angel wings, and build pine-branched forts.
And we find chewing snowballs an addiction
stronger than eating Hershey Bars, sipping hot chocolate.
Snow. Its crust girdles the landscape,
its sun giving up when a blizzard shakes the maples,
pounds the second-story green shutters.
These winds blow nightmares out our bedroom windows.
Refreshed we crave more blinding flurries, more snow,
find new legends as we ski and sled this winter gold.

5

The music box. Seven melodies spill
into the farm house over five generations.
On dark covered days I crank the cylinder
as released oak scents comfort split languages,
its unexplained thunder whirling about
my bed, my growing bones. The yellow-bronze prongs
brush protruding knobs. Tingling notes
ride the room's ablution's breath.
Muggy August noons, bone cold March nights
attach its oak wood box, but can't
penetrate its inner glass top,
a reversed underbelly holding its music.
And we suck its sounds, breathe our world safer,
in tunes floating from this old harmony maker.

6

Let this day bloom silver white cherry blossoms
and have burgundy cover wild strawberries.
Let pole beans give signs in their skins,
and let us be made mortal by garter snake bites.
Let a full moon glow light on our begging bodies
as we worship yet another Michigan lake,
our hands making sand castles on the beach's hide
before we throw away our swimming suits
plunge naked, eager to embrace this liquid caller.
And far to the south of our once glacial carved world,
let penguins dive about Antarctic waters,
the plankton lush, flush with salt.
In all hemispheres nature glistens and babbles
except for upright mammals growing logical.

Upon Viewing 'Night Nude' by Steven Mortz

Lean
boned
erect,
torso
firmed
against
back
wood,
her arms
curve
down
to her
hips.
And
legs
though
thin
are
of
authority.
And
we
go
breathless
as she
commands
her domain
in
silence;
and
woundless,
demands
from
her stance

our salute
to
her
flanks
and
proud
sex

Untitled Dream Poem

I swim the bone of survival,
the hills, the current seas.
I lift the dawn's skirt
where scent
keeps night's memory stored
and washes us of worried stories
we think we must march.

And hosanna begins
as land and ocean bear witness
to new poems floating
through my darkest caves
with the eye of sun
calling me home.

Questions, Lost Blood

1   I find an elm still alive,
then a whole forest, pulsing desire.
I crawl into one moment of their shared heat.
There I see your wound against the sun.

Did you allow my laws
to scrape your songs
lost now deep in that forest?

2   My bed is sweaty
calling to my thighs' illusions
a twin earth
where heat and desire
taste each other, growing
red without confusion.

But did I ever ask you
how your clouds were born,
and how the magic
of one soul
lifted all up to the rainbow's lost seeds,
now in pouches
dangling inside your home?

3   Look, if you must,
tether my voice,
when you search for another skin to lick.
I though will unfold,
and slip into a waiting smooth tissue,
where we could grow
and resolve my memories,
get into the forest of forever,
knowing the force left to die
will record itself in your lost blood.

Chastened

I said "yes,"
and moved an inch forward.
You shed hair from your chest.
I ran to a nearby field
where sentiment
broke from rock,
where corn tassels
without warning
released their pollen
near milkweed pods.

But oh, were we meant
to escape into salty seas,
break water with kelp,
feed that sand's ridged bottom?

My moons now leak;
so in explosions of want,
purple mist floats
toward my bed –
and you are there,
with blackened beard.

But we can't walk again
to live in forest's dark exit.
No one believes us anyway.
No one cautions our words
breaking into the forest's moans,
streams nearby humming disaster.

Send a Hologram to My Stone

Send a hologram to my stone
if there I lie
inside a permanent memory.
Saved no more
but glad of faith
and winter storms that will
scrap my bones
into altars of marigold songs;
and roses for daughter's
pilgrimage into the sea,
petaled flight patterns,
crimson and burgundy heavens,
as she learns finally
her body's ease,
her soul's feed

Parable

I shoved my life of trivialities
and purchased ten stones.
Each had a scar.
Each broke with me into crystal pieces.
When a penniless minister found my cut body
she repeated hosanna five times for my soul,
then crawled into a highway's culvert
to moan for my only child
who would not find me whole
but as a woman
who did live her life in seasons,
in blue and red paragraphs,
in a green orchid pool
struggling for tender tomorrows.

Crow Haiku

two crows on fir branch
showers soaking their plumage
feathers rinsed for flight

God Sign

Sew me a will
on a bandage
marked blood.
Bring me
seven marigolds
propped up and plump.
Call me to your altar.
Stand on its stone.
Stake out
your calendar.
Sign it.
God.

Upon Viewing 'Fallen' by Terry McHale

Leaves on a canvas sheet.
One pile: tree rejected,
earth collected,
we respecting.
Can words transport
these dried
bronzed
yellowed
golden-rusted
images
to our emotions,
for a tremulous memory
a song for the eyes,
fixed on this canvas?

Tree, the creator of these objects,
might stand rooted for decades,
Is it fair that foliage
dissolve into the hungry ground
while its source continues each year?

Autumn, we know, *is*
the last breath,
that late panicked pace,
the tiny drop going, going,
before death takes her turn again.

But I am a maker of questions posed,
of possibilities,
yet stand mute
as the sunlight gives and gives,
as the rain empties its gifts,
as the night quiets the land,
as the earth turns on its axis,

in the darkness of the
galaxy's hold
on our stunned breath.

Renewal

In those days
velvet bled its purple
into foreign armies.
We all stood tall with hate
thinking hell to others
shape our future into a sun.

The vultures knew better.
Their eating scraps just added weight,
not love.
And when we tried to burn cities,
elect our own prophets, the night sky
choked with unclean darkness
and venom-soaked flesh
covered the streets.

I won't share more history
and the summer may still
come unprepared.
But cherry blossoms
surely will have their say,
with fragrant scent
flooding the evening,
mending those exposed
and wounded days.

Blue Invited

Blue, you could be
a gallon of pepper
an alligator's rabid tooth
a forest of withered dandelions
a science fair gone dry.

But Blue,
I see your hazel-blue dawn
your morning blue bonnets
your royal tears below cathedral spires.

Nothing of sun's movement
in your seasoned wind
your near perfect
water soaked cover.

Ah, Blue,
glorious with white paint;
here, no tattered tale of whines
for I find in the soul of you
this rain of loyalty
growing to the stars.

I will follow you, Blue,
if your thunderstorms
shape my gardens
scatter my blood
along canyon's west face;
there to wed
with your showers
there to become
your azure flush
hound to your poems
my home.

Nativity

A poem resides inside a desert's heart
or on the lip of ocean's growing swell;
or in peacocks with rhyme or couplet – hollering parts –
with eyes, a fan created, painting some spell.
Rainbows sprinkle sighs, dreams flower.
Grab every color, take one for lunch.
Along comes a meaty rhyme, taste that power.
Pops into this page. Such a daring stunt.
Eat a favorite from the rose's pose.
Turn into land and sea, our planet round.
The singular letter (dance together) chooses
a star, a chanterelle, a daisy's crown.
Sounds come rumbling, like an infant's cry.
In birth a rhyme sails across the December sky.

Morning

My mind
wanders
through
after-sleep
dreams.
There
I want
symbols
in peach
splashes,
carved
like
orange
begonias.
But
mind
just
wallows
in chaos,
quicksand.
And
dreams
promised?
All
evaporate
into
air's
distant
sun.

Meditation

Wisdom is always threatening
to break apart
into tiny memos
of facts and instructions.
When it crumbles,
it meaning the bony story I try to paint for you,
a new law reveals its structured walls,
its pirate chain of a cold of blizzard memories.

The Isis daughter, though, of our days,
the Ra son also of bone and blood and tears,
are ready to believe,
to seek new wonders.

But if love is what we really want,
then I need lessons from you,
a moon walk around your place,
a cat to guide me
as we test each other's strength
for this moment of eternity;
and learn how the gods too
can weep in joy
after their descent to the dirt here,
the furrowed, luscious rows
in the plowed fields
left holy and damp
from our pink glow of love.

Sight

break my bones
and like
jelly
I slip
into
ocean's
benthic
waters
sweet talk
pelicans
trying to
scoop
me
up

and this
briny liquid
makes me
whole
like
a planet
a mosquito
a blind poet

So Say the Words

Put syllables on tongue
Chew their meanings up
Swallow the dance whole

And walking
Your life feels different
The space around you
Solid
As a continent
As a rain drop

Naiko

The cat sleeps in pain
as AIDS rumbles
throughout
his arthritic body,
resting now on our couch.
This black Persian
shoots pee
from his infected bladder.
Saliva spills out his mouth.

I grip his legs,
hold his shaking body,
repeat softly "Naiko, Naiko".

He has used up most
of his nine lives
as my daughter's legacy and mine
dissolve before our red eyes.

Where is the kitten
my young daughter chose
16 years back?
Where is the peacemaker
we spoke through,
we petted together,
when adolescence
kept tearing us apart?

My partner bathes him
on a Monday night.
Ablution for his next journey?

Returning home on Tuesday evening,
I find his curled-up body

on the back porch,
wrapped up in one flannel shirt
my daughter had held him in,
his Siamese voice resting forever.

And four hours later,
his bones too
rest one foot under
three granite stones
with his play foil balls,
his catnip mouse,
our love.

Warning of 4-25-18

Medicate my meditation
and love will sour the shocked sea
but meditate inside your groin
if you can tolerate lunar invasions.

I will denigrate this plum
you set on my plate.
And no cost, for eradication
blooms by your shore.

But let the tulips conceive.
Impossible?
The concept, the consciousness,
the birthing of wet I know.
But wet you find too
in my sex, where strength
grows to the ancient towers
just under the surface
of your conscience.

Do, though, feel, and pray
the lungs I exercise every minute
can contain themselves;
as my vocal chords scream your birth songs,
the crowning screech in my (still) hosannas
and lauds you may deserve,
or not.

Basket

sold my soul to a tangerine sun
ah, but the gods were happy
I found new love
in a basket of poems
a language of Sanskrit and roses

Let's Rethink

I can not suddenly be here
with diamonds
falling from sky.
(Oh yes, it is snow, but at night
in full moon? Ecstasy!)

I can not suddenly smother the earth
with kisses
and promises of forever,
not after seeing the Grand Canyon,
its womb
open to the universe.

I can not suddenly
break into sweat,
convince a stallion
to gallop
over a cliff,
into dazzlingly cool ocean waves.

I can not suddenly
take you
to an Hawaiian lagoon,
swim with you into Eternity.

But wait.
Let's stop with that last "I can not"
until I slow down,
visualize
eternity and you.

Yes, to rethink,
as waves from a building tide
hurl their crashing,

pounding, waterful mouths
over our bodies
as an invite to forever.

Yes, let's rethink.

Unguarded Heart

For all you know
I'm a beast
growing angels
behind my bedroom door.

For all you know
I eat liquorish
ransack tide pools
sweep floors
sprinkled with rubies.

For all you know
I die every night
licking your limbs
in memory
or dreams
or in your bed
when you sleep.

For all you know
the caterpillars
on your rose bushes
carry diseases,
the rope noose hanging
above your barn door
dangles at full moon.

For all you know
I love you without boundaries
and shave your chest at night
sprinkling every black hair
on my quilt
to pattern and design my sleep.

For all you know
I am a stallion
pawing and stomping
in my stall.
For all you know

I am a silver bullet.

And my target?
Your naked heart.

Fragment Torn

Rose colored noons
crusted the Red Sea

and women and men
devoured by faith

woke to mend the holy trees
and sought like songs

the spiritual, the early
but the womb born,

left upside down,
and pride formed

the grandparents drove
and even swam
toward the pallid shore.

Look closely, or blue maps
dissolve our trips, bent for

soft cries, for sensitive pitch.

Lamb at the Altar Workshop, 1992
~ for Choreographer Debra Hay

Foolish this dance, bodies slithering
one over one another,
roaming under thighs,
around sternums,
making hide and seek
with armpits.

Are we
as two legged-creatures,
prepared for reunion
with trees' children,
a banquet on a floor of mud?

Sweat reaches its apex
in the meandering
choreographer's dream.

"No one stand. No *one* form
to dictate the ahs of rewards"
the priestess shouts.

And I now of no one face or history,
or family battling for smiles,
lick sweat dripping
from dancers' skulls and knees,
tumble into their crashing bodies
to grip my eyes' reward,

and gratefully exude rose scent
through auras dancing
amid their temples.

But for a tenth second's breath
I fall, and history eats my heart
with rabid hound teeth

sends cracked needles
through my pupils,
pushes whole circles out
into waiting
cement mausoleums.

Only memory,
and a crystal ball to paint,
bring me back
to a new face, a new ball
flashing bloody tongue.

Twenty soloed pieces, together,
lower this head, this Sphinx,
into a flooded river,
soak it with trembling hands,
with giggles,
as they find again
the burning cord,
break one with a rattler,
tasting river's new juice.

Dénouement

This, you pronounce,
is the end of us,
the coming no more to
the pride of us.
But endings bring peace
if a popular stance.
We kiss, we cry,
then a latitude dance.
And I was a sailor
before you arrived.
I gathered hummingbirds.
I served honey wine.

But you say
it's the end of things,
the coming to terms
without a swing.
What must I do though
if you fly high?
What can I play
as your relevant style?

I lost you once
with your Aztec tats.
I lost you again
as you grew in them.

Where is my posse
to rope you home,
home, as in safety
and hearthside and womb.

The forests and oceans
breathe in your sighs.

Will they not be able
to adjust your tides?

I live in snow drifts,
an ocean's wave.
I buy ten roses
to cover my stage.
Tomorrow you say
is the end of us.
(I drift into caves
to compose myself.)

If tomorrow *is* the day
then bathe me tonight.
Fold me in red silk
before you depart.
I'll wake up tomorrow
and crawl for my soul,
ask my bone spirit
to gather me whole.

III

Carita
~for Kira

I saw love once
on a blanket of stars
in a river bed
before the new year

I spied love again
on a postcard
in a photograph
the year 1971

I once smelled love
the breath near mine
five minutes old
like chanterelles
sweet
fresh from the woods

I then heard love
inside a baby's throat
crying for milk
for mother's smell
for the lungs of forever

Carita - The Spanish word for "little face"

Possibilities From a Surrealist Mind

What drops itself into a sea of blood?
How do goat horns hear the mountain streams?
Do parrots give secrets out
on their tenth speaking tour?
And whom do you love, on off weekends
as fires heat up the canyons again
but the sea massages the shoreline?

I have bound myself to love
in all its happy and grotesque states.
I have swallowed the moon, only
to find that pies made of dirt and promises
don't settle well in life, or in my most vivid dreams.

I have looked to your burning eyes
more than once these last few years,
found coal and sapphire,
a big hunk of ice cream, all green
and making promises from your pupils.

This has got to stop, this playing
with revelations I don't seed, nor find helpful
on job descriptions.

So I settle into my cushy chair by counting
the crumbs on my floor
left over from a few (and spaced out)
thrilling nights.

But the closing still comes,
the miracles retire, and the sunflowers,
roses, and one sea anomie get off stage,
except, except, that one bruised bone,
protruding from my left hip,

still feeling the beats making the notes
as I cross another mountain brook,
awake to a blazing sunrise,
and the bee's secret language
as it sucks up more pollen
for the road.

Three Poems Built for Xochipilli's Son, November 16, 2017

"Poem 1: 1:30 pm"

I dredge up
my soul
from your loins
and wander through
its explanation.
A fierce joining
of mind and confusion
drains into
Saturday night journals.
What I miss
grows toward a paradox:
a sandwich spiked
with July moonlight
and a portion
of your raw bones.
Yet lullabies still
flood my morning news,
their stories
soaked in orange blossoms,
garlanded tide pools.

"Poem 2: 2:40 pm, a verse"

So many rose petals dampened my bed,
scarred with blood and a clown's frown.
I wept when rising out of my head
as dreams took flight without a sound.

Numbers scattered across my wall.
The engines of memory drove my bones.

Each baked tomorrow began its crawl
toward calendars, healing my new made poems.

Hallelujah I cried, grabbing my verbs
that populate notebooks, language full.
Soon came a Tanager I could serve.
I'd cry it my rainbow, sing new songs bold.

"Poem 3: 4:50 pm"

Meditate with me
on your mother's birth place,
your father's shrouded past.
But believe
that the temple
made from your galaxy
carves its breath
with nine
holy gardenias.

And know well
my feet
will shape trails
through
Mt. Everest mist
when
you hear sapphires
sing
for my dreams.

Xochipilli - Flower prince (in Nahuatl language): Aztec god of art, games,
beauty, dance, and song.

Flight

Stray tomorrows
a broken season.
Departure nears
and I feed my gut
as if empty skies
it senses
won't take
you to safety

where I
could gather
your total being
inside my
night fantasies.

You leave nothing
no phone numbers
texts
selfies
just
airless
endings.

What do
marigolds feel
or blue corn
the cacti
in the desert
when nighttime
has finished
yet the sunrise
still in labor
already has merged
with their light?

Peach and cherry blossoms
drop their petals
outside pasture's gate.
So too, my senses
grow out of bounds
as my hallways
give way to
silent brown rugs
grey soaked walls.

Meanwhile
far across the planet
the bones of memory
too weep;
and I am afraid
as you move
to other destinations
like ocean currents

and free like air
like this world
of no endings
no closings.

Chanson Villanelle

I have a language hidden in the sea.
Its sanguine lungs break wars and poverty storms.
Will you begin my life in this construct?

The blackberries scatter along the cycle path.
Mermaids leap upon the piers nearby.
I have a language hidden in the sea.

The path swings back to hemlock bathing air.
Outside the dusk I find 20 bluebird wings.
Will you begin my life in this construct?

Salmon scented women skip down the shore.
The gulls and terns release air from their throats.
I have a language hidden in the sea.

Four upended waves carve shells for splendor.
The starfish, tufted puffins, connect those waves.
Will you begin my life in this construct?

And I remember how you sang that night.
Wheat sung ocean, foam bathing the stars.
I have a language hidden in the sea.
Will you begin my life in this construct?

Mask

I fathered the hovering moon.
I mothered the canary seas.
And inside the dove a cradle rocked
the tones of a closing stone.

There's nothing to give me warmth
as I lie on the sea's gritty shore.
And stars coming into sight
can't combat the old dreams shone.

My mother has broken her soul
and father has taken the source
for scouring the meadows beyond mist
where storms could revive the pulse.

Arrival

Lemons, you exclaim,
grow in your mouth
because seeds
in the dreams you own,
cry rebellion and spite.
To be though excited
about roses spreading
throughout your diaries
does not heal the hurt
splitting your bones
day after rushing day.

I find though another mirror
than yours.
Here a fateful man,
young in the ways of planning,
but ancient in the blood
carried from planet to star to nebula.
I see your darkness
as evening lullabies,
their music so tender that bark
melts from the toughest surrounding oaks
and their songs move through honey,
their notes stroking faces with dove feathers.

So you see,
hallelujah is here.

Barren

Would I have run
from the sturdy moors,
been my own shining storm,
and you like a snake of love,
your skin diamonded,
dominant for show?

What do we worship
in a palace of moon
and galaxy shows?
My love,
you won't follow me home,
and I won't lead you now.
(Were you once
a tender rose, or a fortune
grown through golden floors?)

Give me your sapphire eyes.
Give me your skin.
I wind my bed
around your shores.
But what, you ask,
of the white stork
you won't find
shadowing my bones?

Let Us Make a Poem

Let us make a poem,
lay out words picked
from a Scarborough meadow,
or from the squeal of a newborn
who took the air to claim
I am.

Let us make a poem,
where our children can eat
chocolate chip cookies
splash around tide pools
play in daffodil fields.

Let us make a poem
to be transported beyond
moon's first light,
where sorcerers, witches and angels dance,
where rainbows color on request,
where Easter lilies sway in dreams
outside our bedroom windows.

Oh, let us make many poems,
and place them on our own pillows,
to be found each morning
signed and kissed,
by our own future sons and daughters.

After Roberto Bolaño

1

I won't break
the soldier's glance
at chocolate being licked
from her breast.
It seems his wooden door
has exposed a moon
for cravings
inside the cave
ribbed or veined,
and painted like
a teacup's bottom.

2

This abrasive wound,
this floodgate of desire.
How can I dance both?
How can I not lick the arrow,
the god my body grows from?
Look, a marigold
sprang from my painting
and flew to nearby wheat fields.
Such an ocean of pleasure.
So broken though by
December's rains.

3

I so hoped
you would feed
my bones
jump out of your shadows
rise from your father's ground.

My craving
now reeks of sour milk
and rainbows
pushing
to free
your wall
called love.

Erebus No More

1

I say *thee* is my stream of crying.
The running brook can't dilate its trying.
The rose is a mystery in the rising.

Sound remembers twigs, the rustic bark.
Pale women casting minnows, slow to sharp.
Salacious memory breaking every stalk.

And underneath this pedal, this piano note,
I rage for holy moments, living coats
of wine-soaked patterns, destiny: the soul.

The circle grades itself: soft round stories
breathe into baskets: the minted glory.
I'll take moon rivers into gentle fury.

2

I'll take moon rivers into gentle fury.
Breathe into baskets: the minted glory.
The circle grades itself: soft round stories.

Of wine-soaked patterns, destiny; the soul,
I rage for holy moments, living coats.
And underneath, this pedal, this piano note.

Salacious memory breaking every stalk.
Pale women casting minnows, slow to sharp.
Sound remembers twigs, the rustic bark.

The rose is a mystery in the rising.
The running brook can't dilate its trying.
I say *thee* is my stream of crying.

Eros Choice

What break she caught
a luminous agenda
outside her frozen tasks
I was asleep
could not dive so deep
as my caves marooned
retreated
as if crusting on a forest moon
as if no opportunity for love
or even love's coastal songs

Family Farm Photos

1
Proof comes in a day, an hour.
The morning glory tightens
around the fence post.

2
I can't explain clinging to a rusted wheel barrel.

3
Down the well, down the stone
drops. This second of no sound.
My sister Kathy
saves us all from falling.

4
A pig stink and grunt at age five.
Two chickens pecking
each others' necks,
blood squirting out.

5
See the angle worms, tomato branches,
corn silk, a decade-old horse bit.

6
Will our swamp pond endure
and continue frog creation, their
eggs safe another year?

7
I dance across
these farm photos,
drape the family hammock over every one,
begin a blessing

in the space of inheritance
calling me home;
and just once,
free and warm and alive
to my mother,
to my father.

Homage to the Moon

Liven up, stars; the goddess/god
shines tonight. And those hills
refracted back these millions of miles
my lust and heart-love bloom in.

Some piece together
the whys of lunar trails,
the scientific perfection of explanation.
I though have dreams coloring
in coral and turquoise
the vast space of time and love.

Look fully tonight
before you pull down your shade.
The stars glitter hard
because moon has reign
and its motionless light
its intense energy floats
throughout your night
so that dawn
looks like just a left-over piece of memory:
cold, silent and taking you to task
as you again defend the day with rubies
and sun power, but with a lunar dance
memorized upon awakening:
pure, ecstatic, full of
yellow explosions
goldfinch splendor
sunflower smiles
in all we erotic beings.

Raptures in Red

I swim through oceans
of raspberry juice,
burgundy songs,
strawberry lipstick.
Though there is
no actual red
to swim in
(except the Red Sea),
I wrap myself in
blankets of scarlet,
taste my ruby sex,
its fire flooding
one impatient body;
and I seek flowers
that can grow
serious red blooms,
like the geranium
or the peony
or the rose.
And the music of sangria
bathes my thighs;
and I am curled up
in a cloaked night
tasting again beet-red
found memories.
And soon merlot
is on my lips
with Paris, then Bologna
courting my tongue.
As I look for
ravaged sunsets,
the curls in my hair
bleed out garnet
or cherry

and I have joined
forever
this red dance,
this power force of night,
this frenzied language
feeding my hungry blood.

Sunlight and Shadows

I am afraid of me
that secret voice
that roams my dreams
that tackles me in late night talks
where I wish for new lovers,
and a permanent friend – woman –
but hopeless by morning.

Yet jacarandas bloom
their fierce purples
for five months running.
Can I ride their set of moons?

Now I come to you,
and wonder about your
shaping precisely
your future ten years.
Such confidence
in your own carving.

Life though could have
other plans for your soul,
even with suns to guide you,
and tattoos to shape your dreams
in the cull of each wave
you try riding
in the sunrise you paint
growing old.

Blood Shame Nexus

I am a feeling barrel of dirty underwear,
used language, a stock set of dreams.
My flesh is tired, can't be kept firm,
water soaked with the tears of shame,
imagined, and real as the well of any nightmare.

Someday a family portrait will drip
memory out its secrets.
Two parents over Catholic
and a bathtub of bloody paint
will clean us daughters upright,
my family's still life hanging still
on its canvassed river.

The River Song

1

Birds, do you peel away at the insects, the larvae,
searching the dirt with your beaks and feet?
Meantime, the moon drifts through the branches,
and muskrats hide out
in the banks' multiplying holes.

2

In a kayak, rounded for my belly and bottom,
I drift alongside the naked roots, their
earth blackened homes, pocked and gutted
by the water's nocturnal floods.
Who sees this land alive and raw,
shifting its shapes,
calling for painters and sculptors?
The tree branches fallen,
design the water's edge.
Lucky for the song sparrows,
the wrens, the towhees,
grabbing the October berries,
naked and wine red.

3

Everyone deserves a boat,
a lunch packed
with peanut butter sandwiches
with bananas.
Everyone should get days for the drifting –
floating excursions
where water and body breathe close,
where the slushing, swishing liquid
speaks to the floating sides,

and all is home with our liquid
meeting its own shores
while the river moves along
looking out to the big river,
floating, floating, floating.

Release

Caution makes
stories white
the bath of bloom
frozen.
So give us plenty:
dancers of corn fields
golding the acreage,
honeysuckle and lilac
staggering our nights;
and babies nursing
full for the meals
choirs deliver
from our lactic seas.

Story

I wanted the wind right.
And the bicycle coasted downhill.

Beside the lake,
and where the water cooled the pickerel,
I swam out to you.

And my dream of that day,
collided with the pavement's chuckhole,

where blood dripped from my knee
and bravery was a story,
far away.

Black Widow Morning

Were you on the *inside* or the *outside*
of my screen door in this cabin
when I first saw you before breakfast?
This detail is significant considering
your reputation on my list of spiders
to escape.

But graceful. When I tried to coax you
to crawl onto my leaf, your fragile legs
alternately touched and sensed
that leaf, before backing away
from my invitation.

And perseverance.
I gently tossed your body,
attached now to a twig
(your obvious transportation of choice),
at least four times down the embankment;
and after every toss
but my last, you still started back up,
sure no doubt shade was available
on our upper pinnacle.

Would I have treated you less kindly,
if I had known your identity?

I know there's a wolf spider living under the sink.
I thought of cleaning the whole area out
a few weeks back, but didn't feel adventuresome
opening my cupboard door
to a webbed world. And glad I didn't
destroy that sticky silk bed,
as it kept a good lid on cockroaches
and stink bugs populating these rooms.

Were you IN my cabin, Black Widow?
I haven't slept well the last few nights,
yet thrill at stars all bunched in black sky,
the moon setting with its shine brightening my face,
and the darkness after.

Have you also kept me awake,
my subconscious alert to your presence?

I leave you on the hillside,
unless of course you crawl back up and again
get to my screen door, or closer.

Oh my *Latrodectus hesperus*,
arachnid of my nights,
my red-hourglass-bellied female,
please depart!

To Love

Pull me out
of creation's nest,
make me beg
with blood
on my feet,
for night's
black
holy
dust.

Give me a map,
where over
high cedars,
beyond Atlantic's
gnarled shores,
I find dreams
from tribes
singing
to skies.

There I offer
my selfhood
in exchange
for glacial waters,
for king snakes.

There I beg
in horror,
but kiss
air anyway,
to love
to love
to love.

The Hag of Beara's Plea

Rope me down these rutty rivers
I pray to the heat of the moon
Continue my language for the deep blue seasons
Confirm me you yellow-bound song

I'm dealing my jangles with a new found freedom
I'm posting my lips to your tongue
For the talk that you deal
From a level-headed meal
I sell to invisible suns

Language conspires to dope my muse
Kicking her body through duty
I explode no schedule
I am sentenced by bulk value
Oh Sappho, break hyacinths, bleed me

Leave me afraid, King Snake, Yellow Frog
A cup of black fever for the road
Crushed scattered bearings
Hidden sweat, Mother's language
Cardinal shocked, green words, fractal soul

Warnings Carnate

It could have
been Lake Michigan
eating at the dunes,
an April morning
west of our farm.

It could have
been a night star,
damning the rage
that spilled out,
a breast fallen
from its parched lip,
and then, and then,
the crashing lake's
moan.

You see,
it could have
come after my last birth –
a warning to love,
and love,
and love
the tender eye lashes,
the tiny feet curved,
the voice gurgling
after the breasts.

(But could it
have been you,
telling me
to walk that scaffold
and yes play
with the policing moon?)

It could have
been my fate,
to laugh on a dot;
and loosen whatever figs,
kept breaking with leaves,
their bouncing earth rings
ready without grace.
But I kept silent
like a plowed field
where furrowed rows
lay straight
and one funeral
passes by
and one passenger
feels heat
from an
unmarked grave.

Son of Xochipilli

There you were,
inside
the sweetness,
and darkness,
of your eyes.

Your pain
touch,
your intimacy
clothed
in each cornea,
each floating
above your face.

And my face
touching
this.

And everywhere
was poetry.
Everywhere.

Dorland

1
Break Away 2
      -for Chery Jean Vasconcellos, author
      of the poem "Break Away"

Got to get to the coast of my blood
Got to holler me down
to the spine of the desert's wind

And to the curve of the live oak's bent river limbs

Going to trash my steady days
Want in?

Pick a match
and strike for the flame

Now let's get moving
to hot Vega,
and Deneb
and Attair,
galloping

2
Waterblade

We came to a tender
Moment of grace

Sweet and even was that place

The tree's hide
The corn's glistening eyes
No snake beaters carrying chains

A well named Waterblade
fed all the land

So parched, we raced to its hole

Memory sat pink
inside each gulped drink

Home
Our madness
Linked

3
Dorland Grove

Trunk in brown ink rivulets
Cord ridges
Limbs to 60 curved feet
Girth huggable
Encrusted sap
Charcoal black
Remains of leakage from amputation

Nuthatch, squeaky pitch hummer,
Hops up one stub
Bags larvae and bugs from crown

Sun trails
go through
groin's dying crack

4
Rejoice

A sheltered rock lies still
in the bosom of pond

Meanwhile, hummingbird
stamen sucker, frenzied and forward,
sunders my bedroom wake

I, sandwiched sister,
had *not* a moccasined heart
to bake and crumble
a January's iron weight

But now memory –
delicious stairs, resin drenched

Feed, a woman's edited dreams
with fruited hands,
bloom sweaty desire

My trusty maples crack tales
and open in dark amazement

5
Girlchild

The girlchild swam high
under my January mind

Don't let them spoil your baby skin
your language of butterfly breath
in this land of respectable lens

(The fields parted for her under wind)

Float, child, to the breasts I tend

Yes, your pencil boxes bring
Your pony, yes, guard friend

6
Dream

The sickle moon
dropped down from the sky
stole the lions sleeping in my mouth

Drought made me gasp
wound words left

Oh hush, firefly suitors,
too late for your love
Build another cactus nursery
sown in my chest

They, thank god,
wrestled with this source and its suns

Stroked all syllables
Breath sweet

Now my hope
Our mighty course

7
Bond

I bring through this land a child
torn at the edges of its bones

Me, the unborn daughter. The hiding breasts

We walk a broken life.
Cross wooden blocks tumble out

This lullaby, drugged and painted,
means azure eyes push hard
to reach cerulean gods

(Words, get to the quick!)

No peace in the diaries, and unborrowed wolves,
tamed, bled our home

You. Future
With kite and sword
And hummingbird, our tireless bond

8
Rose Moon

When I am left to bury my life
and leave March showers to fill my grave
the rose moon may appear
Sit on a western break of Draco's tail
and believe me while I howl and whimper you
coyote's dawn

Moon won't reply
Smart moon, and wily, for my fingers
call battles to this page, not lunar sweat

But hold me still in your sourless glow tonight
We can chew pieces of bread
baked through the drought and folded seasons
poured on my days

Rose moon, a couple stranded
Bring their bandaged lies to tornadic conclusions

Ruby language and vows of cream,

unlied,
sweetened

9
Forgive

The season grows down to its mother's back
(We laugh like angry monkeys)

Such are the sounds one mother bakes

Get me to the naval of matter she shrieks
(Soul desire, the harpoon's fire)

I made me a ring of rosaries, of tree roots
And we took care of us all

Oh mud mother I pulled you out of shining disaster
I gave you linens for your grave
My scars wrapped you in leaves

Tears again in love's shimmering stream
gave me my name from your blood
What is it you want from your western altar
from your new roaming home?

Pale moon,
drifting,
unborn?

10
Homecoming

I come down this awkward season
Weary of frozen lies

Look to the sky, language grunts
(The husk of a broken mind)

Yellow with feathers
Laughter
You distance yourself away

Moltened and weary, I succumb
Blaming that fiery sky

11
Home

Flash me a dime
oh prison soul

We can buy stories
hidden in chiseled code
That's how roads drill into homes
The third pig's bricks didn't shore it all
Rivers seep through mortared wall

But Sweet the taste
I cook big bad Canis Lupis a steak

Born in a den this second life
Fur
Sun
October wine

12
Milk Snake: a love story

Like a tooth caught in one vat of wine

Tell me of lactic desires

Breasts Oh ambrosia Oh sweaty sweet skin

And the coiling body, the nipples' land
Make a mammalian feast
Food in the manger Slurp love

You, god, give me white blood juice

Here, my lips
Here, my wrists

Nest of babyhood. Year of caves and memory
We found our lambs, bandaged the fire grown at birth

I found you twined in the rescue hold
For love loves a bite and one year trapped and growing
Oh milk snake, please me in our bed's sacred sheath
Split, can't bloom

Yes, the fanged touch, the tooth

13
Departure

Would you take this nectar
how could speech be born?

A laugh dissolves down my well's spiny throat.
Morning glories shut still at dawn.

And if no dented mattress,
no sweaty breath in night's holy abundance?
A chalky volume of silence
choked into blunted days.

Linger and make your time a magenta river.

My rivulet body
Shores
to gather us home.

The poet was a participant at the Dorland Mountain Arts Colony during the summers of 2000 - 2003. These poems were created in the first year.

IV

The Agon of Love
        ~ untitled love poems

1
Morning comes fast,
and quick burns the calendar.
Inside the eucalyptus,
I hear a heartbeat
drumming your name.

It is too much!
The butterfly
drifts over the canyon,
the hummingbird
eats the air,
and I try
holding back memory
of your muscles, tattoos,
crashing
my dreams.

Where are my places
to anchor,
the ravens to talk with,
the sunflowers to harvest?

Time gets dragged off
this aging planet.
I float on moments,
and sift through new relics
for your box marked promise,
nestled in this poem,
waiting.

2

She said it once you know,
at the bottom of the stairs,
fingering the light switch
as I walked through the front door:
your name, spoken, with measured sound,
to her mirror first, and then to the potted clivia
where orange blossoms still hung from two stalks,
still in bloom these last several weeks.
I didn't want to catch her:
the heavy silence following,
her prior promises to stop it, finally.
She did turn to me though, right before
pulling away, and the after silence,
that continued scraping her daily.

And did you think it worth it,
that moment of wonderment,
of muscle memory dancing so fiercely
that the river drowning her in muck
years after, did not stop
that moment, that slice of second
from the flash she allowed,
she welcomed,
of your soul walking
into her cells that night?

You will never know
as you walk your days,
alive but in confusion as to just
where and how
you find your own future,
sown now on the back
of your Aztec shirt,
painted in green and black
and shaped like Eagle, watching.

3

Where do you go
when you leave your apt.
for errands or mind healthy walks?
What monsters do you keep at bay,
what lists do you follow?
Where do you find T-shirts
that showcase your Ivory skin, black eyes,
reveal in slight contours your muscles,
display your Aztec tats?

I have less roads to travel than you.
But their girth,
their rubble filled ditches
with stink and dead roses
crack my bones often.

And my belief
that more are growing,
can not be gotten rid of easy
as I wake up so many nights
and find a hallow dragon
dragging itself across my porch
with yellow arrows,
fractured unicorns.

4

Sometimes the cast is cold,
the players disappear under icebergs and sand.
I have a reason floating in my bathtub.
But it melts too soon
and I forget, sudsing the memory from my limbs.

What games we act
to forget the tears,
the joined laughter,

the music of our bones,
met to be united
and carved for eternity.

My fig tree grows to its girth in weight;
and its leaves and bark celebrate
the morning's lungs and scent.
And from this giant I walk the city, adopted;
and warm for new decades I live.

But memories must wrap their blood
and ivory musk around my days;
or what is there to live,
if seeing your eyes fade into a morning image,
fleeting and gone,
before I figure out why
the gasp for breath,
the cut air losing, losing?

5
I set my seed in the ocean's groin,
a place of wealth and sorrow,
a dance of the whale and plankton.
Believe me, the elements
carve my memories
and siphon blood from skin I wear.
What fruit will I grow
if the kelp slip into these pods of me
and the starfish grasp hold my mortal thoughts
breathing the sand's wellness?

Enough I beg my mirror!
The marigolds will soon come;
and their scent
will be my morning ointment,
my evening's erasure

of all things
mercurial,
greenful.

6
Is this the blade of my being,
the spike in my orifice;
the cunning warrior now in tears,
my sword bent backwards,
my uniform in blood?

I write these lines
knowing you will never see them,
knowing the ghost in your dreams
you will throw away, disgusted.

(I have crawled through the darkness
of women's breasts in my paintings and poems.
The women too will never believe me
as I paint their sorrows and bursting memories.)

I run to the news,
try folding papers over and over.
Is this gravity turning my lungs,
scraping the corn's last kernels
onto August mud that won't dry?

I step down this gravel road,
pick up stones still lying over tar,
over the engine I want to squelch.
God, does the ache never stop?
Do your tattoos, muscles,
never leave my mind?

I must find a well,
one in Eire's land,

where waters
cool my heart,
where its power
can attack this disease
and bury Eros forever.

7
Thought I could do it, you know.
Thought I could move his dance
into mine, a bit.
Thought the gods saw my soul
bleeding with affection and hope,
for bathing this special one
encountered so briefly
three weeks ago.

But Large Spirit has other plans
for the river
rushing
through my bones,
walk,
language speak.

Yet what do I do
with black eyes
soaking in kindness,
and beauty
captured on one selfie?

--The odds are not even
on the charts!
But is Einstein's proclamation
about imagination
to be discarded,
beyond reason,
for even

one single woman's
desire
for the sun?

8
What comes of this wanting,
this passion so brutal,
that blotting out, forever,
is what we beg for,
if unobtained, if refused?
But moments later,
or hours,
or maybe a whole a day,
the want, again;
yet the heart's hole
getting bigger!

Who made the rule
that the skin, once tasted,
the muscles touched,
the breath, imprinted,
and oh yes, the eyes, the eyes…
break apart the body, psyche, soul;
so that swimming lap after lap,
gorging hot fudge sundaes,
singing in your best tenor
the song
that ripples through the audience
and brings many to tears,
won't stop the bloody ache,
that memory in your bones?

Grief dissolves briefly
if a mountain pass –
powdery snow drifts
glistening through January sun –

comes within reach;
The pain can subside
as you soak in this lush alpine.
But too soon,
ecstasy looks for a partner.
And there you are,
back to him.
The gods, the great seers,
all claim this too will pass.
But do we really want it gone so that we what?
Walk paved routes for paychecks,
suck in the daily news,
play computer games with strangers?
A balance?
Just some kind of syllogism:
dry as an old turnip,
and as cruel.

In our dotage I guarantee
one night a star will appear;
and we will wonder why
it shines so intensely
as tears again soak our heart,
as a red rose
we had not noticed
in bloom by the park bench,
now dies
in the October dusk.

9.
I could be a sequoia
a Coho salmon.

I could bleed royal blood into a canvas.

I could hang up a poinsettia,

crawl over its petals,
sing to the fence's edge
it looks over.

But I, in loving all of *you*,
go to the water's lip,
coming straight out of a glacier,
brown from gravel and earth;
with a piece of deer antler
crowning the flow.

I circle above your head when I dream.
But why the scars on my thighs,
like sacred pebbles
from those same dreams?

The voice of the northwest woods
begs for my heart
while you sleep in the cacti of your father's land.
And you moan in bed
after your drinks,
too many to hold up the brick walls
that hide you from your birth.

And was he there, your father?
Did he see the blood
and hear those same moans
of your mother in labor,
on your delivery, before he ran?
Oh he, frightened, could not have then
touched with wonder
your baby toes,
traced with his finger
the tiny line of black hair
curving down your back.

But
I
just
love,
and follow your bodily form,
which for now,
is chiseled in black ruby,
and breathing out
a golden musk
of dawn.

10
I can almost smell your sweat,
you live so close,
(yet hold faint memories of me).
I pound ocean shores:
sand cold and hard,
and sun
burning my face and arms.

I want to escape into bed each night,
dream of butterflies, Ferris wheels,
dinner with close friends;
but the weight of a stone
pulls down my heart,
the rock that bears your name,
that settles in, uninvited,
when night descends.

Do I beg the past to come back?
To change so that you
would *not* have knocked on my door that night,
that I would *not* have let you in?

I have not had a god of your beauty
come into my bed,

of all my years a woman.
So why now,
when my skin so quickly wrinkles
and my body leans toward
the swaying trees of November?
But you are not to blame.
It is my heart that insists
you again cover with honey
every cell on it.

Some claim I am lucky
that you,
my young Xochipilli,
gave me rainbows and roses
and poems, still pouring out.
Next week though I say enough.
I will write an ending
for this brief one-sided affair.
But until then,
the heart drags itself behind me
as I look to the sun for help,
for its brilliance of sight,
and for my place within it.

11
How is it we see energies
in violet moments;
but not the black phoebe,
when homed
in an aging palm tree?
Look, fish to me your skin,
your black Irish blood
though camouflaged
in Hispanic genes.

I shall cease this burden love.
And believe with my sweat,
my uncrushed memory, that you
skyrocket your soft hands,
(oh silkened dove);
where the river's currents
lick your thighs (lucky ones),
and carry you
into a banquet of moonness,
yellow flavored and full of god.

And sorrow of the old gods, the shrinking gold;
but gold *is* old, gold disintegrates
into its dollar smells.
And shall we now dance,
sourcing the land's grand heart thump?
No, go for the corn tassels'
powdery sex,
and the pond's silken cover,
and that whimper,
tender bells of the birthing infant.
This I live for, or crawl defeated to my dumbed death;
for morning glories make new blossoms,
as sunrise climbs over pines,
as I search in my bed for love,
and love's naked voice of want.

V

The Rose

There is
a rose
drinking
water

and afraid
no more;
calling the

crimson moon
to aide
in its
unfolding

where
words
grow.

And bone
folds
around
the earth's
shell

as blankets
cover the
unowned
sun, and

breathe
tomorrow's
poems
into the rose.

Dew of the Sea

~ for my sister Rosemary Ann Insidioso
(July 23, 1937 - January 29, 2019)

Sister, do you come into this land
through a July rainbow,
to grow your gardens
with fairy tales, college degrees,
fierce political stands, familial love,
so your children, your grandchildren,
can harvest these gifts?

I have been wandering in a place
where mountain's hemlock became
my moment's nurse; and
I, catatonic still, in a white barn
whose door flaps against baled, molding hay.

Sure of nothing, I walk now into noon,
and there you stand
holding a wired bone,
tapping your head.

Stay honorable and with love, you command
and then this happens: a song
gains power in my voice you grow.

And purple roses
you scatter
on my doorstep.

You, now holding nothing, nada
you, shaping my new earth.

Rosemary - Latin for dew of the sea.

Creation

She said
no more blues
He replied
as a mother
as a sister

So began
their roman seed
baked from
river's groin

So began
first waves
of creation

and peace grew
wide and strong

White, With No Apologies

Tastes like sweat on a church pew
after divorce is refused, or
like breakfast mush in prison
where a guard picks his nose,
takes protection from the tenants.

And to hear white? Like anger
caught in a toilet bowl,
or cellophane
after its shelf life has terminated
and the shelf caught on fire
and it landed on burned strawberries.

You smell white in a wasted day, or
a love letter sent to the wrong address,
a guarded house where wall safes reign.

I get a whiff
of the gray variety in tax increases,
in that collective breath
leaking from political mouths.

And boy you better believe
white looks like corporate spit,
or maybe the brains of a dying poem,
a sword swallower gone mad.

The Stealthy Mountain

leaked into my third dream
and silent as a grave, shadowed
nearby elm and maple.
The sky drooped
and the clouds ducked
behind the firs.
Before dawn
wolves escaped
under the briars.
And the barn's red door,
crooked from winter storms,
flapped awake the rooster
who had crept behind
layers of huckleberry bushes
watching with one turned eye
its own last act.

Blue Slant #2

Blue, like hope on a baby's smile,
the medicine we take before dying.

Blue, like the Red Sea,
before its history, before
Biblical stories are born.

Blue, like the plague,
where it is over, and the living
crawl out of their homes, rejoicing.

Blue like a bath and
the fresh skin in it.

Blue, like desire for the bed,
or the drink, or the shaded willow.

Blue, like the doves, their wings
planted on an oak branch
their eyes, drawing the land clean.

Blue, like rivers
and seas
and lakes
and ponds

like your mouth,
mine
traveling the universe.

Inheritance

Maybe my wanderings
down jeweled worded phrases,
maybe this leap
into fresh white blank paper
is after all, my mother's will,
put together before her birth,
like a set of guidelines shaped
from blood type and a blue moon.

And I can be a cowgirl once more,
hogtie the dreams spilled
from her photographs,
that carefully sit in baskets
along my daughter's bed,
where I see a story still in its making,
a heart thumping her golden trails
into the stars.

I Am Loaned to You

I am loaned to you
from breakfast
to next dawn,
on courses in love

and your acreage
expanded, will bloom
where your corn
bursts into fields
of hybrid men.

Grow all you
for me and
for like women.
We will lift our breasts alike.
We will bloom fresh crying
in your sight.

And great the task
of crawling with hungry joy
your torsos and fiery limbs.

Oh bleed your heavy muscles
for us on this erotic plain
of honest lust.

I Lay by a Cedar Trunk

I lay by a cedar trunk
wonder about desire
sinking so low
into my gut and beyond.

Yet in morning rituals
I decline visions until the sun
can shade dreams still lingering
like on a pier of granite-patched holes,
of that water beneath
slapping itself
against the wood posts
and gurgling from its trip
around a boulder's sacred home.

And I want to free you,
of fears around numbers,
yours and mine,
uneven on this planet.
I want you clear-eyed in revelations,
in moon messages,
because I can't get all
or any of what I dream of
when night has taken control
and stars a solid yellow
bleeding the sky.

Poetry Making

We somehow think a poem
can't grow without pure sight,
or hours sleeping for strength.
We *think*. That word
sometimes so broken,
so bloated,
with scum sickening
its own field's breast.

On waking to conscious thought,
one might break the poem
or stop its skin, now wounded,
from coaxing itself to breathe,
to strain to grow;
and we punish its worn edges
on a piece of shoreline,
where it is simply
waiting for the dawn.

But there you have the poem
with letters that crawl
from its moss and maple roots.
There the poem; and inside
our confused heart,
there sometimes too,
a piece of the rhyme,
a mat where syllables
grow their secrets:
a circle of saplings,
oval songs.

Clarion

Let me bide time
with chickadees
with monarchs
with sprouting crocuses
in snow beds

In this circle
this cave of care
I beg young people
to let their bleeding cease
to seek their songs their souls
from western cedar's breath
from the eucalyptus skin
and the brook's clear flow

and afraid no more
of their own
awakening roars

Make Me a Poem

Make me a poem
a source for magic shows
crimson roses
1,000 dollar bills

Paint me a poem
where horses cantor
through oceans of white foam
where their breath, their sweat
soak my dreams

Carve me a poem
of western redcedar
with wild strawberries
piled high on its porch

Dream me a poem
a string of orange marigolds
packed
inside its sun

and I will grow
into eternity
loving forever whoever you are
and journey into tomorrow
with a backpack of souls
all brilliant and alive
around this circle you bear
this miracle you find
in your own hungry soul of want

Oh Glorious Yellow of Imagination

My love eats desire,
for eruptions of the new.
In this tide of want,
this fistful of galaxies
spilling out his soul,
he finds
gold miracles.

A Sanctus encircles
his new moon's voice.
Daffodils strung
along a hillside's path,
silken their petals' home;
their stamen
dust his lips,
he, now Eros blind.

He cries for a
lantern's yellow glow
to fire his starving nights.
The air splits wide,
pollen bleeds on
his belly, thighs
until
like the dawn's caves
he dances a
wild churning.

And later sleeps
on his own loamed earth,
at rest
from this sun soared day.

Three Suites

1

I was growing my seed
when you broke corn.
Kernels nourished in
my bottom soil's dyke.
Your fiction moon whispered
in breaths of daffodils
regarded as talking bones,
from Crone's nourished throat.

Speak through green moons.
I will cherish your young songs
worshipped with old beliefs
of sandalwood dawns.
And shaped toward
a peaceable dance
of remembered poems.

2

The sound of moans?
Of gnawing rocks?
The blueberry's sweat
and coffin lid clicks?
How can forgiveness
come asunder
in a moment of grace
of bone wonder?

Oh moon
hold us all dear.
A circus of beauty
combing us free;
and breath
collecting inside
our dying thunder.

3

Steward me toward
cupid's pranks
and juxtapose this romp
with blood, still,
inside my confused
my coffined dreams.

Pleased and shocked,
my people
of the broken sentences
will start howling;
and again afraid, then
dancing high
through their sea's
new tongue
I have woven them.

Sonnet

I saw language covered in a storm,
black stones scattered along its shores.
What had bound itself in a moon's form
now wilted, drifting along our earth's floor.
But can't you see these words, soaked, yet safe?
I sing watching them float about and melt.
Turn here, turn there, greet their visiting place,
their whispering syllables you and I have felt.
The sun won't come until I have spoken,
given their emotions a chance to live.
But diamond studded sighs become broken
and stranded voices fill up a moving ship.
It passes, it bleeds our mouths for hungry words.
Its drought remembered inside our remaining worlds.

Defining Ecstasy

Sweet is the territory of desire.
A rose is not lost in its definition of scent.
Through the pupils of children
can the world breathe again.

Take a brook found at its source,
trickling out of itself, born under
the earth's skin.
To come upon this baptism,
in childhood, one June afternoon,
helps shape risks
hungered for in later years.

A mountain outlines the horizon,
hope suddenly crawling that mountain.
Then that hour is a moment,
an explosion of newness,
of bright yellow, fierce red,
pulsating with energetic revelations
to carry on maps marked ecstasy.

Lick Me Orange

Lick me orange growing to the moon.
Crave my seed, my lavender blooms.
Bisque this heart I wear it grown.
Make me into purple stones.

Dandelions blush, look to their roots.
Tight mango starch, a canopied dirt.
I side swipe twice your frozen tongue.
I give you insight, and diamonds to touch.

But rhyme jails me — stuck — tangled in form!
I dance, clouds break, maybe fresh songs?

But free me quick from these iambic beats!
I give you black walnuts and stars for keep.
Whee, I escape, we jump that metered fence —
but cry, for my poem lost
in the free verse trench.

Pilgrim

I seek the scent
of the May sun
and the flowers
that eat its rays.
These blossoms
spill their own
blood
melting
my garden
of stone
where its very
breath
was once
bridled
with the dead.

Wheat Field

Trudge toward that gold you see.
Ripened and free these last hours,
the field is a glowing furnace
eating the plain's August heat;

and you, sister, brother,
need bushels of warmth
for your winter nights;
and your dance through this grain
could bloom into precious dreams.

So hurry! Gather to your body
these bearded stalks.
The land soon will be shaved,
a stubbled earth
cut down
to its dying pours.

Are There Circumcised Roses in Surrealist Paintings?

I grow, and like
just becomes silly.
Fun, the darling, the miracle sky
will strip bones, and this is the freedom
I paint red; and sing
before noon, before angels
fawning for my brilliant breasts
my sexy brains
over and over repeating
"The cake's growing chocolate
and you are invited!"
Namaste.

Dictionary Revision

The dictionaries have it wrong,
words defining words from other words,
their ancient utterances
tossed into adverb bins.
And though sound is emphasized
for pronunciation
among our sister/brother humans,
it loses the mystical,
the old gravitational zings
floating through space.

What forms, what structures
make their way into a lexicon
where grief and ecstasy break
into regimented steps for explaining
one versus two, he versus she
red versus black, and so forth?

We must make word guides
with sounds gathered
from whale sonars, from rocks
splitting off from pinnacles.

Maybe a hoof print
or Monarch dust
will create greetings
on verbal post cards, dug up
in boxes buried millennia back;
a new screen to widen the days,
make hearts repositories
for love, and galaxy smiles.

Try it in your shower,
or by a peach blossom
you hear open at dusk.

Poem for the Millennium

I thought I had world's answers
when one shaky day a wilted cedar
facing my house, leaned toward my roof
and scraped it raw.

I thought I'll pray again
but be a devil in disguise,
seize all burning believers
from the pews of filled churches.

I even half believed my voice,
its quaking tenor fooling the rapists,
those legal ones, and their assistants,
who arrest prostitutes, when I
hauled them all into my own court.
The jury, fifteen females,
ages two to hundred.
And you can imagine the verdict.
And every guilty party
forced to grow roses on the planet,
work seven days a week,
thirty-seven years.

But hearts cut by the pound
mend only with intense dreaming,
and with a garden where sun
stitches heart together
through its blazing heat
and pansy and marigold surrounding
this miraculous surgery.

So my chest took these lessons
of mind, the I thinks, supposes,
and if and if, tied like a sailor's knot,

and raced to ocean's smile
to give her the entire package;
and ocean's tongue licked
the edges and pulled it
toward her with foamy she paws,
and I, left on the beach,
my eyes and heart scraped clean

River and Land

the land moved toward the river
found a raging torrent of language
a home dug for confusion
hiding in river

and land saw palm trees floating crooked
moon in rage, daughters flying; and followed
river's bridges, its shores, its uncertain maps
to the plowed and sagging furrows where land stopped
between land and river's ribbed and chapped face

(a life gets sweetened within the jagged rock's sounded stream
and mounds can be smoothed of pocked remarks
of ornamental damage anyone sees fit to carve)

the land faced the river, and remembered the river's
gifts, stroking the rivulets and quiet ripples
the pearls of the river's skin
knowing how quickly a rainbow could melt the bonds
forge river's crying language
leaking into the land's pressing loins

the river found the land and in land's layered dirt
of bones and binding secrets
of sounds flooding its belly
released the bellowing songs where river must live
where land made home a trust
linking the river's birth with land's gardens

Question

Fresh dandelion shoots,
you have braved another winter
from seeds guarded
inside earth's coat.
How is it you can muscle yourself
through dirt and weeds
yet accept the sun
to harvest your gold?

Bound

I could just touch you
and screw the foggy moon
oh betrayal grays
the lemon's early skin

like our romps in tight beds
or musty showers
or where floor boards leak
and moldy photos promise
"good vibes at the prayerful diner"

Plea

I go alone to shape virgin soil
keep my own blood dripping
until its mist floats
toward a mountain's gully
In illusion I bark
my soul's soiled voice
Softened eyes though
bathe its soloed and petaled memories

Will you dance with its bones
Will you lay hosannas on its mouth

About the Author

Born and raised on a fruit farm in Michigan, surrounded by woods and fresh lakes, and from Irish/German Catholic and musical roots, Pat Andrus lived briefly in Long Beach, CA and then Rhode Island for two years before settling in Seattle with its rich northwest flora and fauna.

For a number of years she was adjunct faculty at Bellevue College after receiving her MFA from Goddard College. During her many years in the northwest, Andrus was, for a time, an active member of the Red & Black Books Collective; became involved with poet, Pesha Gertler (mid-1980s–early 90's) through the organization *Women's Voices and Visions*; served as Artist in Residence for Washington State from 1990-92; assisted as manuscript editor for Open Hand Publishing; studied dance in the 1990's with choreographer Debra Hay, among others; and partook in artist residencies at Dorland Mountain Arts Colony (2000-04). During this same period she gave birth to and helped raise her daughter Kira, along with Kira's father and stepfather.

A new resident of San Diego, Andrus hopes to share her life-long love of the arts, and her strong conviction that not only does the making of art, in whatever form, bring more hope to our planet, but its very expression is the closest connection we humans have to the divine. With this, Andrus is a co-facilitator, with Crystophver R of Poetic Legacy I and II, offering free monthly workshops in San Diego to introduce walk-in participants to a wide range of poets and to encourage generative production of their own writings. She plans to continue writing and disseminating poetry in San Diego.

BLUE VORTEX PUBLISHERS